VALID, VIRTUAL, VEGETABLE REALITY

T0160153

# valid,
# REBECCA
# virtual,
# CLOSE
# vegetable

WINNER OF THE MELITA HUME
POETRY PRIZE 2017

# reality

 **EYEWEAR** PUBLISHING

First published in 2018
by Eyewear Publishing Ltd
Suite 333, 19-21 Crawford Street
Marylebone, London W1H 1PJ
United Kingdom

*Cover design and typeset by* Edwin Smet
*Author photograph by* Anyely Marín Cisneros

*Printed in England by* TJ International Ltd, Padstow, Cornwall

The right of Rebecca Close to be identified as author of
this work has been asserted in accordance with section 77
of the Copyright, Designs and Patents Act 1988
ISBN 978-1-912477-20-3

WWW.EYEWEARPUBLISHING.COM

For A, L and M

Rebecca Close is a researcher and translator based in
Barcelona. She graduated in Philosophy from Manchester
University and has a Masters in Comparative Literature.
She is the 2018-2019 fellow at the Centre for Arts, Design
+ Social Research, Boston, Massachusetts, and a recipient
of the Hangar/Casa de Velázquez artistic research grant.

# TABLE OF CONTENTS

# THE
## MELITA HUME
### POETRY PRIZE

Rebecca Close is the 2017 winner of the Melita Hume Poetry Prize.
She received £1,500 and this publication by Eyewear Publishing.
The 2017 Judge was Vahni Capildeo, whose comments in part read:

*This is a distinctive, urban voice, which holds on to speaking and feeling throughout states of fragmentariness. Through the fractures in its language, perceptions, and experiences, things still truly matter. This is evidenced in the habit of thorough delicate observation that translates into the ability suddenly, and aptly, to evoke a pastel dianthus or a satellite signal, or to draw unexpectedly on earlier, traditional forms without falling under their yoke. It is evidenced, too, in the engagement with 'secondary worlds' of film and other visual art, not ekphrastically, but as part of processing everything: the various figures, situations, scenes and would-be-meanings cracking with violent variety, unassimilable chasms in friendship, unnameable proximities, and tender moments of weird connexion. Even if you have not lived lives resembling those depicted here, whether their worlds of work or experimentation, you know that these lives are aspects of yours. As the Melita Hume Prize is for a first full-length collection, it seems good to award it to a book which made reading feel like a fresh adventure.*

## FIRST MEETING OF THE ARTISTS' UNION IN BARCELONA

little red ball of taste accompanies espresso
callous raspberry served, its fake
'please dip for taste'
*are you kidding me* I kick the stirrups
gallop through the rococo style restaurant
giving diners the finger, stealing lemons
from their toothpicks for my sippy cup

it began when we found the shale tooth
I can't tell you exactly where
definitely at the curve of the road
where we uncovered the clue
dusted off the earth
with our little dig brush
proof we would need wigs
proof oil is moving backwards (first time then being)
we picked out blue dresses
to baffle the surveillance system
stumbled down *la rambla*
spreading rumours about our barrenness
and how we were depressed
(we sort of were) we plucked our old jeans off
found something new
a coin in my equestrian boot
a pussy in my shoe
little eyes like twenty-five imbued in the wallpaper
*we're watching you*
with our fifty limbs we're coming for your air miles
your furniture will fund our movement
(we had wigs on, which enabled us to ascend to positions of great power)

I don't know compost from art
but I know what money is and what the weather feels like
I bite hard on my mouth guard, start spinning
*I don't want to wait by working I don't want work to be wanting*
I want to get paid for everything
every time I move towards this paranormal radio sound like
*waaaaaaaaaaaaaaaa wuuuuhhhhhhhhhhhh whooooooooooo*    it is me
who is delivering your cucumber by drone, delivering
your cucumber by self-driving car
I want to get paid for that

searching for the address of where you are on maps
you find a list of things you have done since 2009
written by you it's only 30% true
when we speak on skype our bodies are our voices
a person is a number
of sparkles going out quicker or slower, you are
everywhere
green, red, gold        blue fading into dark
I am holding you
colours of the evening
colours of Christmas on TV
our souls are the TV no one watches anymore and
Christmas is the art
sometimes the news is on
sometimes you watch and watch and watch me

# THE PASSION ACCORDING TO A VEGETABLE

## (i) an emotional plant

*I'll waste none of your time with contradictory advice.*
Virgil, *Georgics* (Book II 45–46)


Reader, You are King.
Make this easy for me.

Imagine you are wild again.
Let hair tumble down
the hills of your shoulders. Let
words river through the crumbling clods.

Hold your native components together.

It's time again to put the pill beside your plate.
Rub your face
with a little heap of grim ashes.
You are a spent field.

It is true you should take the pill.
It is fact you should open it.

There is much to gain by setting flame,
watch the colours arise.

Don't spare yourself heat's word, either because
all fire engenders a weird productive force or because
fire purifies our failures.

There you'll find the hidden ways of nature.
Stare in open-eyed amazement at the breaking news
*We want to keep going!* England says,
sweating,
injecting Nubain.

Is numbness also required
to keep up stamina in poetry, I wonder?

Pour a mix of seeds and seashells into parallel lines.
Turn the sod. Leave the grass and mud
upside down, like the subject.

The subject is inconsistent,
as it changes it leaves no trace.
When I try to question it or question myself
I get boiled, salted, baked, oiled.

## (ii) self-portrait as a microphone

sitting at a table
waiting for the flogging
what is the difference
between remaining calm
and functioning at a basic
       level
can take most of it
from gunshots
to dialogue
have no sense
of volume
but a thousand eyes
for classifying
how intensely I feel things
sweet
scared
these are things that can be measured
also the *timbre*
textures that are familiar or unknown

# (iii) the passion according to a vegetable

## (iv) Fausta

At the base of the day is an onion bulb of white noise.
In the apartment room, a screen breeds internal wars
in every mind consisting of two kinds of violators, the
rebel man and the military man. They fight to the death
to get their clenched fists into the sky. Their fists always
pierce red or green skies. The knobbly gold body of the
Oscar statue floats between hands on TV. In the United
States, the enlightened pray standing up. They give the
Oscar to film directors like Claudia Llosa, whose second
feature project, *The Milk of Sorrow* (2009), was the first
Peruvian film to be awarded the prize.

We watched it on a cheap copy version and realised at the end that all the scenes where the main character (Fausta) shows the potato growing out of her vagina had been censored. Without those scenes, the film doesn't make any sense. The words on TV are divided between red and blue. You have to sit on one side of the tram to hear the red ones and the other side of the tram to hear the blue ones.

Fausta's mother was raped by soldiers while pregnant with her. The white noise in the room is also the moon, discovered by the whites of my eyes. I see it from my window, open in April. I name it in the language of power: *moon*.

The film's title alludes to the film director's belief that fear and suffering in a pregnant woman may be transmitted to her newborn through breast milk. Journalist Carla Salazar explains in a 2010 article on boston.com how Claudia Llosa, a distant relative of writer Mario Vargas Llosa, got the idea from Harvard University anthropologist Kimberly Theidon, who researched sexual violence in seven Peruvian farming communities in the 1990s. Salazar writes, 'women told Theidon of their fears that children born or nursed during the violence might suffer psychological disorders. "They said, 'These babies are a bit slow. How could they have been normal drinking so much pain, so much fear?'" Theidon said in an interview from boston.com'. In the film, fearful of suffering the same fate, Fausta places a potato in her vagina as protection against assault.

I hold something growing in my mind and at the same time, I wonder if I am really thinking when I'm thinking. You asked me that once and the fact I'd never thought of that made me feel nervous.

Instead of the scene where Fausta shows the potato, the screen flashes black. Now people can't even say the film is a bit 'magic-realist'. Fausta, played by the actor Magaly Solier, is inhibited and soft-spoken, but overcomes her fears and opens up to the world through a gradual and difficult process. I check my mails on your laptop, a million stars on your desktop background.

The sky is crushed, the sky is printed, the sky is broken open. I look into my hands, each finger a family photograph, glossy like frozen pizza.

Theidon said in the interview from boston.com that, 'The great thing is that it has elevated a bit a topic that nobody wanted to hear.'

I touch the keyboard, I know the messenger, swipe the dust across the window.

We can't decide if this is a good film or not though. Isn't it true that if something wins the Oscars it's because it upholds offensive premises? Like some babies are a bit slow or women who live in rural areas are inhibited and soft-spoken and must overcome their fears.

## (v) in which we pay for our domestication I

core to knees
panning technique
see jigs
in god's pit
get once twice
three times
stitched
or vault chores
where cows chat
only chatting
pot for tat
taste it
O heaven
snack aches
lapped up
one of us is dog
one of us is ruthless
*shh shh* woos the room

## (vi) in which we pay for our domestication 2

the flesh
of the mango
is sweet to suck
its firm green skin
when ripe
protects it
when it's hot
or is pushed against
it splits
juicy
but it's bruised now
you cannot sell it

## (vii) the jelly the water the chyle the chyme the humours

the house
the rooms
the steps between our rooms

        trails of bathwater
        between our rooms
        routes I take to name parts of you

a toe emerges

ten toes rise to the ridge

the toes go down
into the water into the tub I am alone
        I walk the edges of my room
        then go straight
        into yours
        our ears are on fire

the bathtub warms with hot water
        it cools it drains I get out
        the party is downstairs
        william dafoe turned up last night
        I missed it as I had to work

when I got home the drops had dried but the trail was there
and the footsteps between our rooms at night
        what is the divide between you and I?

I saw the ghost
      he was dressed
      as a magnet at war
      dirty shoes
      cowering on the steps beside my room he bowed to me
      he was angry

Ana is cooking garlic and potatoes in the kitchen
'Boys Don't Cry' is playing downstairs
the drinks arrive

people call out sometimes in the old people's home next door
      the crying sounds are quite distressing
            the nurses come to comfort them

      the sound remains

nestor came to stay he gave me his necklace I lost it

monique left yesterday I spent time with monique

            *it's the parts they leave*
            and I really thought you were leaving me
                you leave

I found out later it was a hospice

      a passing place

      I watch a series on my laptop

it burrs clicks
sits
hot on my stomach
lap
      balances
      heat on my chest
          the left side
of the bed is hot
          the right side
          of my body
              is burning

          our love is old
          a telephone wire
          crossed and letting
          partings in

# EPIDEMIOLOGICAL-TROPICAL HOMESICK

*Tropical thinking is obsessed with proximity, it spatializes, it
maps [...]. Epidemiological thinking is obsessed with transfer, it
temporalizes, it simulates [...].*
Cindy Patton, *Globalizing Aids*

A lumberjack shirt dries on the clothesline
between houses in the good neighbourhood.
My body is the good neighbourhood. Brother,

don't jump. Mum's coming, I'm calling her.
Come down from the edge
of chemical transfusions of the exteriorising particle.

We push our firm bodies up against theirs
to get firmer. We go down to the kebab shop
to watch the fight in my mouth. In my mouth

we are the last people up and we live here.
A hand touches the sun through a skylight,
brushing a wind chime of weathered glass.

Whose house, whose h-ou-se is this? It's Thursday.
I put on a lumberjack shirt. Take it off. Hang it up.
Take it down. Put it on. It's raining worlds.

What words? What us? The sea is drunk
with his green beard. There is salt in the sea, salt on my lips.
I drink salty tea. Whose party is this?

Being here or not being here takes such imperium over us.
The effectiveness of the campaign is in making us think
blood is water and water is blood.  The importance of the road

is the density of traffic in search of gardens. Brother,
we are blooming into something in a garden,
bordered by hedges that meet in lines that make a grid

that the searchlights show up at night.  A healthy mind
is a body in transit, wading through
provincial swamps,
skyscraper fogs, sparkling sandwiches,

looking for proof.

## I'VE TAKEN IT ALL IN AND I'M TRYING TO KEEP IT DOWN WITHOUT IT COMING OUT AT ONCE

Package tape taping barrel edge.
Head touches lid. Soggy packing tape

doesn't stick the lid down. Messages
decanted into envelopes. Lick the edge

down to send it. Spit swelling, spurting
over microphone, through the tape.

One in every home. Towel dripping speech
shaping audience. The most complicated organ

is the audience. Three parts: rural, suburb, inner.
Licking, *beep beep* in my hands. Kissing you

in the street. Traffic of saliva through the town
transforms the width of ducts:

tear, tube, auditory. Hands in my water tank,
sealing it. Love's a dangerous word.

The electrical variation of what I'm trying to say:
*three small bones*. Everything drilling

in the city. Couldn't get back to the flat in time,
police were there. Door boarded up

with wooden planks. *Timing* says cockroach
on the curb. Rain comes unplanned, in patterns.

## (viii) gardener's world

January:

In Optimistopia people gather in the cinema to watch two films by the early twentieth century French Film Director Abel Gance: the first is *La Roue* (*The Wheel*) from 1923 and then *Napoleon* from 1927. However, after seeing *The Wheel* they decided to abandon the screening program.

February:

In *The Wheel*, a woman who grew up beside a train track is led into a marriage with a disinterested landlord who refers to her as 'my little train lady'. The reason her otherwise loving and supportive father encourages her into this unhappy union is unravelled over the film's nine and a half hours. The girl was adopted, but does not know this. Her father found her in a bundle of sheets at the train station, where he works. The daughter is the epitome of spontaneity, loved very much by her brother, a charming violinmaker. She wears pre-coloured yarn dungarees with a flat cap, puts the cigarette in her mouth the wrong way round and goes *choo choo* like a train at the party, making everyone laugh. The siblings are often seen chasing each other across the house and tiny garden, which is beside the train track. It becomes clear that the father has persuaded his daughter to accept the landlord's proposal because he has unresolved feelings for her and would rather she leave. He is also envious of her relationship with his son, who does not know that his sister is not his sister. The daughter's name is Eleanor (I think).

March:

With the absence of Eleanor, now married off, the father grows sad and eventually goes blind with guilt. He loses his job as a train driver and is forced to take up a position as a mechanic in a mountain town, where the train passes once every three days. He is, by this time, very poor, living with his son who travels to the city every now and again for work. The son appears busy but otherwise lonely. Eleanor cannot take it much longer and decides to visit her father and brother in a desperate attempt to escape her marriage. This is the father's chance to make everything right.

April:

The landlord, sensing threat, follows Eleanor. He manages to overtake her to arrive first at the father's house in the mountains. He is about to knock when he stumbles outside the window falling against the pane. While nursing his twisted ankle he overhears a conversation between Eleanor's father and her brother – it is the conversation in which the father reveals the truth to his son. (The audience gasp). The violinmaker, feeling angry and betrayed, runs out into the snow heading for a cliff edge where he usually goes to play his violin. He is unaware that the landlord is pursuing him into the white.

May:

Eleanor arrives at the house to see her father with his head in his hands. On hearing the news, she runs out after the violinmaker, unaware that her jealous husband is already ahead. Eleanor runs fast but she's too late, the two men are finishing up their brutal fistfight. The violinmaker is wedged under the landlord who uses his last ounce of strength to roll over and push his rival into the precipice before he himself takes his last breath. The violinmaker falls into the freezing oblivion, his body a pebble burrowing a blue tunnel in the snow.

June:

The audience in Optimistopia is in dismay. Eleanor is heart-broken. The father is grief-stricken. The charming violinmaker is dead.

# VALID, VIRTUAL, VEGETABLE REALITY

my

here / yes /

my behaving luck /

my legally blinding / hanging on

to its job / thus department meetings and /

*this is not a matter of choice* / Donna, Marshall & Roy

has been / attempted merger of Ana / all the stuff in her desk is gone / today suits

feelings / and I've got some / I've veered & aggressed / when I learnt how / I'm

gonna / O / my team were subjected to downsizing / our personalities are children

/ who know for sure now / when he slammed the car door / that Dad is mad

41

## POSSIBLE EMOTIONAL ANATOMY OF THE
## SO-CALLED DECLINING

I try to relate to this conversation
but directly observing
the dead arm means touching it.

> monsieur bayard invented the camera before monsieur daguerre
> but failed to get funding from the government.
> One of the earliest photographs is his
> *Self-portrait of the Photographer as a Drowning Man* (1840).

> I do not think I am a symptom
> though the eye has tried to kill me,
> I fight with him in bed. I am only interested
> in my emotions in as much as I can find them online
> in thesauruses. The places to be
> disappointed or euphoric. But no one likes to be reminded

or surprised. Things spill
from your pocket, arrive
in the room before you do.
People stoop over

for fear of contamination. Chains of associations:
self-portrait of a drowning man; ophelia; hair.

> I saw an exhibition about the history of the asylum.
> Fell on my knees, demanded there were more labels.
> It was such a mess. If there is a man he operates as a cleaning agent.

You get more money. But what is a man?
> The skeleton that prays.

The skeleton that says
sorry

for knowing what you know through touching. A word
touching you is an arm. Don't try to read the invisible
through the visible. Don't turn on the nose.
What frames the eyebrow but the actual eye? david beckham's haircut

gets up on stage to apologise to all haircuts that came before it.
Someone was disappointed
by family then euphorically made a new one,

this is how we do it. kurt cobain's hair
his distribution of lesbian looks. Properly citing
italian men from the movies, I put hair gel in my hair.

My wife loved it. Strands of hair
seen through a microscope
turn up tiny passports to illness. sylvia plath proved she was a man

when she killed her wife. But she was the wife.
usa, britain, argentina. Divided.
Right now, a mouse punches a cat.

That's how unnerving haircuts can be.
The secret of success is always working with the same people.
And I've tried.
I bring a photograph to the hairdressers.

### (ix) I don't want to edit your power-point presentations anymore


I lifted up my eyes and looked –
behold, queer plankton on YouTube.
  The sea angel crawls and glides,
    moving at the mercy of the changing currents.
(Now I'm ready to close my eyes)
  It dodges the lines of predators,
    knows where the edge of the collection jar is.
(Now I'm ready to close my eyes *C'mon*)
  Its body is a beryl,
    its face a strike of lightning.
(I want you here)
  Its limbs gleam burning bronze,
    its limbs are fused as a wing.
(Now I'm ready to close my mind.
Now I'm ready to feel your hand.)
  Its delicate encasing is tightly coiled –
(I lose my heart on the burning sands)
      when the chemistry shifts it lets its body go.

(*C'mon*)
  It swims still.

Am I a type?
Can you find me in the smell of the sea?
In the forming sediments? Am I a common shape?

# CLOUDS

*Where I go, there are always two guards watching. You have to bring a partner and if anyone feels uncomfortable you can call them out and they get removed from the room. Their partner also has to leave –*

Dee, Matthew and I were standing by the flowers. Maya was home and had gathered us at her Mum's for her birthday.

*Romantic partner?*

*Doesn't have to be, just someone you trust. The fact that you have to leave as well means you have to bring someone you know will be ok –*

*Basically as soon as you get in the sauna you are consenting to the experience. So, drugs, sex and hours and hours. It's difficult to know what 'no' means in that context, or when to say it –*

*Is that ok?*

*I started doing this when I was about 14 or 15. I went with an older guy who I'd met at the ponds, so someone I already trusted. I think about how easy it is to find out about these places now so young kids go alone and take drugs and have this really intense experience. What I remember is that if you drop out –*

*What do you mean?*

*Take too much. No one looks after you. The chem-sex thing is really big now, there's a new place on Dean Street that deals exclusively with that. It's good that there is that support –*

*Yeah, it's true that promiscuity is sort of either idealised so no one talks about consent in these spaces or the practices are totally pathologized –*

*Yes,* Matthew said. *I personally wouldn't date younger guys now but that experience was really important for me. At the same time, and I have never been raped, there were definitely moments that I probably was like I'm not totally sure what's going on –*

I started talking about Thatcherism. Dee responded with another description of her sex parties. *We should say that while we are making this distinction between heterosexual and homosexual we know we are appealing to categories of identification that were invented in the nineteenth century* – Dee and I nodded at each other. *Totally.*

*This focus on sexual identities means that we are still not talking about sex, hence the risk, the violence we are exposed to. We need to talk about how we are having sex not only who we are –*

*That is so true.* I nodded again.

Matthew stretched out their hands high into the air and bent over, pushing their hips out behind them in a kind of dance. *I'm going to get another drink!*

Later, when we were filling up bottles for the cab ride, Matthew was laughing, talking to Maya, looking over at Dee and I and smiling, *they totally talked me under the table!*

I felt a pang of rejection.

I spent the night talking to Dee about her new job. She was working for a national newspaper's style magazine, doing interviews with Hollywood stars. *It's about empathy,* she said, *empa-th-issssiiin-gggg,* she shouted again over the music.

We found ourselves surrounded in the middle of the dance floor, people pushing us around as we danced. Dee shouted, *yeah, I felt kind of annoyed about that as it's like O women think too much they are always theorising or something.*

I wasn't sure. I have often been accused of trying to be clever. We used our bodies to carve out space in the crowd.

When we got back we flopped on Maya's bed. *I love this group*, I said, *my favourite!*

*I'm glad Dee came out.*

*Why wouldn't she?*

*She was like not living anywhere last time I saw her. And before that, rehab.*

*Shit. She looked great.*

At one point in the club, in a continuation of our earlier conversation, Matthew turned to me, *you can come with me if you like. You can't come to the saunas, but we can meet*

*on the heath.* I'd nodded, *YES!*

\*\*\*

*Going to see this tomorrow.* Marielle sent a screenshot of
a day's program of workshops and a talk by a famous
French philosopher, *come!*

*I'm sorry, I'm sorry!*

*It's fine, it's just that I'm actually always on time.*

*O me too! But the bus diverted.*

*I hope we don't make a scene when we go in.*

This seemed so out of place, *make a scene*. The force at which Marielle could occupy a space was equal to that with which she would withdraw from it, if embarrassed. Other people's confidence is so arbitrary. Our encounters are often structured by unspoken dares.

I listened to the philosopher's talk as if it were a long poem, which made it easier. I closed my eyes, let my mind wander through the nightmare. A white silicon baby floats past. A robot steps through the window of the seminar room, crouches down so as not to bang his head on the ceiling and, with a tennis racket, bats the jelly baby. *Technology has corrupted the baby!* There are two caves. Out of the man cave emerges a man doll. Out of the woman cave emerges a woman doll. They float towards each other, tapping their plastic bits. I opened my eyes, *this stuff is so creepy!* Marielle was giggling.

A woman put up her hand. *But with the patriarchy, I mean how do we do it? What should I do? It is so…*

She paused and looked out the window.

*Hard sometimes.*

The philosopher's response was long. She repeated the words *self-affection* many times, which Marielle and I quickly gathered had nothing to do with masturbation or writing. The philosopher also recommended yoga.

*Now we'd like to ask everyone to do a cartoon drawing of their apartment with one modification, in response to the term 'living together'.*

*Let's go.* Marielle looked at me, *can we?!* I pleaded. We slipped out the back. In a supermarket nearby we picked up some wine and wandered into the park opposite. It was around 2pm.

*This is where I sat with my friend after we saw this amazing film by Ellen Cantor. It was so funny! It was my favourite genre: low budget, all my friends are in it, nothing happens.*

*O yeah, that is so great!*

*The film made us feel so great as nothing at all happened, there are these banal characters who just move through the city and after we came and sat under this tree as we were so horny and open to the world.*

*You're taking me to your erotic tree?* I was flirting. I told her what happened on the heath.

I was supposed to meet Matthew but when they didn't show, I decided to go anyway. It was 3am. The heath was alight.

I wrapped my scarf tighter around my neck, moved slowly, felt the bark of the trees. I stared or smiled at the women who strolled by, picked up a curl of orange rind from the floor, threw it away, settled on a bench.

Despite the languor London gives me, I was galvanised by night. Sometimes a breach in lethargy delivers an arrow of affect. A thought, some bit of text repeated, moves me. My lips move. Once at work I leaned against the stone column, my right foot in a black boot making small circles on the floor. I turned around, pressed my body up against it, felt the cold marble on my cheek.

*O yeah,* Marielle intervened. *I've felt like that all summer. I've had like three people tell me we can never sleep in the same bed as 'you know what will happen'.*

*That is not ok! Why are they trying to limit you?*

I got back to the heath. Someone swerved across the pavement and walked behind the bench. Their hands hovered just above my hair, then came down softly, guiding my head forward, then to the side. By the time I saw her she was already fifty meters away. She turned around and smiled before disappearing across the green.

I was about to follow when I noticed another figure coming up the path, solemn as a corpse, passing through the pools of amber street-lamp light. Yellow, blue and dark green, yellow, blue and dark green, the figure flickered, advanced. I couldn't see her face until she was sitting on top of me carefully undoing the buttons of my coat, warming herself, the heat burning the hoar frost off our shepherd skin. We'd looked each other in the eye, never

said a word, never kissed.


*Did you like it?* Marielle asked.


*Yeah, I did.*


*It sounds like our lives though, don't you think?*


I looked into her bright green eyes before lying back in

the grass. I watched a cloud cruise into, envelope, and

pass through another.

## (x) untitled

A historian trained us to activate
the inanimate. We were always approaching things
to see what they would say.

We wanted them to say stuff about us
but they said random things we didn't understand.
It was nearly impossible to transcribe.

In the evenings I would drink.
When we lived beside the river Guayas,
I'd watch the surface turn red

with the four numbers
of the year they died. I feel the weight of centuries
smothering me. You woke me up once

in the middle of the night,
to tell me a dream you had. They were making you
dig up the buried, who'd been buried vertically.

And now they are going to speak.

## (xi) adding the details left out of the original message*

mouth bone              burning rock            gets

jurisdiction           hauling syllables       fingers tend

to streamline        the crunching of      keys

I lost you

germ

as a worker

there are cosmoses

a switch

transmission is an archival matter

exhausted by the bitten wind

the mind flicks

cartilage unfurls

in the grooves of reasoning

practices flower

in radio shapes

they mistook it for nature

set it up against orifice

listener as the worker

her tongue clicks


I add in the details


graphics flow coherent

echoing the usual

market twists


towns turn inward

the route darkens

the volume of everything left

*A woman called Uly, who worked as a runner on the 1995 film *GoldenEye*, wrote this poem. After conducting research around the Puerto Rico Arecibo Satellite – host to the fight between the protagonist and an evil agent – she discovered a team of scientists had used the satellite in 1974 to transmit what they considered to be the most important human data into outer space for communicative purposes. Their binary coded message included the numbers 1-10, a few atomic numbers, the formula for DNA and a drawing of a stick man. Later, she came across the work of North American artist Joe Davis, who made what is considered one of the first works of bioart. *Microvenus* (1984) is a genetically altered *Escherichia coli* cell  containing a visual icon (the ancient Germanic Rune symbol) hidden in code following the same binary principle as the Arecibo transmission: the image was converted into 0s and 1s and then developed as a DNA sequence.  In a 1996 journal article, Davis explains why he selected the ancient Germanic Rune symbol, which is said to represent the earth and female genitalia, stating, 'I wanted to add the detail left out of the original message.'

## ARTIFICIAL FLOWERS

*1. The decoration*

our days are entangled   its flower is my
flip-flop    budding from the hotel's wooden floor
its back a black petal gathers filament
legs      filament arms
it crawls the stalk (my strap) & falls   its limbs curled
electric blue shoe what will enter its flesh
it can't distinguish vital data from the
extra parts     I feel
sad the beetle died and confused to find the
airbnb I'm staying in is my own
body gentrified at sixty pounds a night

*2. For just four more nights*

in the garden women isolate forms   appears
the scent of their weaving lives     their rough knuckles
their parted curls the smooth-edged lace of their words
paisley carnations
inverted mother's day     running through the veins
of the soil   presbyterianism appears
god I'm so hungry     we fight in a forest
and you storm off
you see a beetle beside your shoe     it's me
and you love me for that    time in the office
is far from sweet     I've been weeping from my
guts since Ana left
she's just that kind of dianthus with petals
stippled with pastel colours     now there's no one
to defend us     as they make eleven new
suites for biotech
and that's death     to become like the rest of them
I think how artificial my life is   like
sixty times a day     all is ornamental

*3. You are pretty resilient*

you buy me flowers   bright sober trances in
loom-in-escent gardens    enter-sing my flesh
sound-glyphs & picture-phones    just a little now
stars above our heads
I dream in hybridges    two pence a pack     text
within reach     it's better to be a glitch than
lonely to be wild     I love it when you say

# THE PROJECT

Freedom, meaning
the absence of
impediments of motion.

      But motion is obscenely exaggerated in flying.
      An illusory feeling of imprisonment, when I fly.

When I deliberate
      what to do next.

      Each rejection
      of a possibility. Each lunch.

      Every time
      I watch a rom-com.

      This is the winning visa, works
      if you steady your hand, if you look him in the eye,
      if you don't concentrate too hard on hoping
      for benevolence at the border
      while considering how that is the actual opposite of hope.

          We move like magicians
          but the officers came.

Flying is the expedient of motion. The airplane wants liberty –
      the power to move.
      As when a stone lies,
      as when your mother lies (fastened to her bed),
      as when I speak to myself – *It's ok, it's ok,*
          *it's just like a bus going up and down.*

As when water speaks to itself, *I can make high waves*
*I can rush downhill*
*I can plunge foaming and gushing*
*I can rise freely as a stream of water into the air in a fountain.*

I am doing none of these things now
and am voluntarily remaining
clear water with you on the plane leaving Frankfurt.

With my head pressed against the seat in front,
I paddle the reflecting pond of the past. A quiet guaranteed by
the fact that
marriage cannot marriage backwards.

I read a book: pleasurable and difficult
or certainly out of order
when seen from the perspective of the continuity of the airplane.

The book and I watch each other
like new friends: *I want to dominate you,*
*I want you to dominate me.*

The chain rolls on and on then breaks,
when one of us falls
into the ocean, blurring the words.

All that actual space created gets erased.
As nothing was written down.
As nothing was produced.
As all the choices were in life and not in the text.

It all makes me recall the subtitle of a magazine article
I once didn't get round to reading: 'plummeting from the skies,
a project
struggles for life'.

# EXERCISES IN MEMORY

when asked what I'd like to remember
       I said our haircuts swinging in the dark

I'd put them on those nylon strings
       from design exhibitions about the power to stick things together:

pritstick, velcro, programming

       the metal table from the café-bar with its cheap silver
       metal chairs

would be there

       no one puts their hand flat out on a table during a conversation
       but I'd have the moist imprint of a hand
       and the small circle from Magda's elbow

generated

just to communicate we are here
       crisps & beer & pavement I'll never write a poem about WW2

       it would sound like London
       slurping a milkshake where the milkshake is the whole ocean
       it would sound like a rug lifted up and dropped
       the only content of a radio show called *World*
       it would sound like my grandfather
       inviting Maya to sit on his knee at my 18th birthday party

over coffee you said you're glad to see my face
       looking longer & fuller

*you'll be happy in a few years I took so many photos of you*
*I got your best years*

among the collection of super-8 films recovered from an attic in Birmingham
there is one featuring a little dog running around the garden

round and round jumping in the flowers
tugging on Christine's trouser leg

if I was made at gunpoint to write a poem about WW2
I would make an audio recording of this film

and have it transcribed

I smiled: my best years are coming

on the shiny metal table of my memory
there'd be a recording of
anyone's voice
amplified
from a speaker you can buy for £5

reading the fragments
I remember now

of the poem I was translating at the time:
*y hay una luz que se apaga*
*realmente sabemos todo sobre el petróleo? Tod@s nosotr@s*
*cualquiera de nosotr@s*
*la pelota encima de lo cual*
*estamos*

**(xii) this is the first account: there were neither animals, birds, fishes, crabs, trees, stones, caves, ravines, grasses, nor forests, there was only the sky – the surface had not yet appeared**

As the object embarked on a vast period of transformation, attention turned to its first great forging. The hero attends a student party where the moss-grown rocky walls and deep precipices are an enigmatic presence and guests discuss their minerals and shafts. Eventually a photograph shoot entitled *Miss Chicago and the California Girls* erupts on its feudal shaping. Some guests argue for a threshold in the accelerated means of technical intervention after WW2. Another gets stuck on a tragic birth, which burnt up the surface causing essences to withdraw under the crust where they rage in emotional recesses hidden deep in the belly. Others argue it burst forth from subterranean realms through irresistible elastic forces accumulated in the movement of plates. Some point out an icy age that scattered parts behind closed doors & privatised pleasure: *her coal black hair, her diamond eyes, her ruby lips, her pearly teeth.* For all of these theories, it came into being catastrophically under conditions of heat or chill, love or war, introducing the question of technology into the study of feelings.

## (xiii) I respect these people so much as we all live next to the cemetery in this city

There is a street
called dead street.

> There is a monument
> to a surveillance camera.

We are not sure if it is critical or celebratory.

> There is a language that is and isn't mine.
> There is a part of me where the sun hits the pavement
> for 200 meters,
> we call it *devil's patch*.

If I were a container and not a microscope
through which the movement of pathogens
could be traced across borders,
I'd hang around on street corners

> naming local phenomena. I am a water tank
> brimming. If I speak I require inspections
> by the Rockefeller Institute for Medical Research.

*Doctor, doctor, I seem to have reached the limits
designated to me.*

*The water is drinkable*, she responds.
The water seems to regulate the scene. Tomorrow I'll leave.

I know you'll leave me soon as I am very obsessive
and arrogant.

*I'm happy,*
I said to tall buildings.

*I'm writing,* said the Sun.

*I started billions of years ago.*
*You just don't know how to account for it*
*as you have only ever considered changing the rules,*
*never the game itself.*

*But Sun, what could be more outside of us*
*than the laws of contagion?*

*You're right I cannot conceive.*

*Let's write to our countries. Tell them we know what you're up to,*
*selling us stories about how we met:'Just a couple of snouts searching out*
*degraded industrial areas,*
*folding napkins at dinner parties to blot the bite.*
*Tiny flaps lifted for hosting and drinking.'*

Wait, what is that link between mosquitos and vampires?
Is it Peter Pan, is it manifestos, is it Tropical Medicine?

*The regulation of markets.*

*You're right, I cannot believe.*

'Buzz around the room a little more'
reads the prescription,
which I confuse with the description

of the future.

It's always failing us
or we fail it or something.

I'm happy,
which is another room. Or the privilege
of choosing
who you pay your debt to.

# SKETCH FOR 'X' AS EXCESS

Size (the realm of the present).
Content (the territory around which we are 'x').
Colour (blue).
Bring up the lagoon we walked around.

Memory: I can't remember what time of year it was.

Epistemic territory: water trapped in a basin.
We were in excess of it, climbing cliffs.

*I thought we were going to die.*
Love:
something you walk around.
The blue lagoon.

Frame rate: 4000 (so fast we can't see it's not a movie).
Holiday pics:
upload them in an array;
a folder marked 'location data'.

The seasons
are not the universe
they are *in* the universe.

Find spring as (x), where 'x' is being born. Find
summer (growing); autumn (ageing);
winter (dying).

A revolution: the seasons trapped in a basin.
Take them out of poetry.
Put them in a museum.

The volcano shakes.
Background becomes foreground.
Time rises

as steam; an ellipse.

## THREE OF YOUR SHOES AND THREE OF YOUR MOONS (OR A REVIEW OF 'THE PASSION ACCORDING TO CAROL RAMA')

I

We're in Dani's car going down to the river after eating chips
Sweet martini winds down our throats
The car's wheels comb the road
Our teeth
remain un-brushed from the party the night before
Our hair is medusa-like
Dani locks the car I shout up to him to throw his keys back
*You're always forgetting things! Your wallet, your keys, your shoes!*
I want to get my face cream
for after the river dip
a frosted white glass pebble pot
heavy in my rucksack
like a segment of moon
His keys have this little shoe
on the key ring You say
*I used to have a similar one*
Dani's is a sandal with a red leather strap

## II

I drift under blue moonlight
I am diligent   a crater
soft rubber moulds
where my wheel face turns
it is your shoe
unlaced
on the tarmac couch
I wish hard on the edge
of its steely toe
silver
it seems a useful thing to walk on   to walk along

III

We are being public in the museum
a geometric moonscape embracing Carol Rama's paintings
I'd translated the catalogue and repeat the words to you
*snakes are not phalluses they are snakes*
*bicycle tyres are not phalluses they are bicycle tyres*
*dentures are not vagina 'dentata' they are false teeth*
*but the organs could conceivably function as a shoe or a brush*
*something on top of which to walk*
*something with which to paint*

# NOTES

'First Meeting of the Artist Union in Barcelona'
'We're coming for your air miles' references the
line 'we want your house, your job, your frequent
flyer miles' from Lesbian Avenger's 1996 *Manifesto*,
which I have often read aloud with the arts collective
Diásporas críticas in our workshop on feminist
manifestos. Thank you to the collectives, artists,
students, poets, teachers and activists who joined us in
those pedagogical and performative exercises between
2014–2016, particularly Noor Afshan Mirza at
no.w.here, Radio Nikosia, Josebe Iturrioz, Leire San
Martín, Ana Longoni, valeria flores, Fernando Davis,
Mariela Scafati, Fatima El-Tayeb, Tjasa Kancler,
Dani D'Emilia, Daniela Ortiz, Alia Farid, Fernanda
Carvajal, Histeria Kolektiboa & Degeneradxs, Centro
de Documentación de Mujeres Bilbao and the Institute
of (Im)Possible Subjects, as well as the texts' collective
and individual authors, whose work continues to
inspire and sustain.

'The Passion According to a Vegetable (i) an emotional
plant'
The title references the 2015 exhibition 'The
Passion According to Carol Rama' at Museu d'Art
Contemporani Barcelona, curated by Paul B.
Preciado and Teresa Grandas. It also recalls Clarice
Lispector's *The Passion According to G.H* (1964), which
recalls the Bible's 'the passion according to John or
Luke'. The epigraph is my translation of the line 'non
hie te carmine ficto Atque per ambages et longa exorsa
tenebo' from Book II (45–46) of Virgil's *Georgics*. It

was inspired by two previous translations (see: Trans. Peter Fallow, Oxford University Press (2006); Trans. Arthur S. Way, Macmillam & Co. Limited, (1912)).

'(iii) the passion according to a vegetable'
This image is a version of an image produced using nag_05 (a computer program which collects and recombines material from the Internet to create a new website or a new image), developed by net artist Cornelia Sollfrank and programmers Panos Galanis and Winnie Soon in 2017. nag_05 is a modified version of nag_04 (realised in 2003 by programmer Richard Leopold), which is developed from nag_03 (programed in 1999 by hackers Barbara Thoens and Ralf Prehn); nag_02 (Luka Frelih, 1997); nag_01 (Ryan Johnston, 1997). Thanks to Aarhus University colleague Winnie Soon for drawing my attention to it in 2017.

'(iv) Fausta'
'Fausta, played by the actor Magaly Solier, is inhibited and soft-spoken, but overcomes her fears and opens up to the world through a gradual and difficult process' is excerpted from, Carla Salazar, 'Peru film on sexual violence nominated for Oscar', boston. com, (25 February, 2010), http://archive.boston. com/ae/movies/articles/2010/02/25/peru_film_on_ sexual_violence_nominated_for_oscar/ (accessed 20 September 2018).

'(vii) the jelly the water the chyle the chyme the humours'
The title quotes Monique Wittig, *The Lesbian Body*, Trans. Peter Owen, Beacon Press Boston (1975) p. 28; 'Boys Don't Cry' is a 1979 song by The Cure.

'Epidemiological-Tropical Homesick'
The epigraph comes from Cindy Patton, *Globalising Aids*, University of Minnesota Press (2002) p. 48; 'The sea is drunk with his green beard' is my translation of the line *'el mar borracho con su barba verde'* (see: David Ledesma Vásquez, 'Aquamarina', *Cristal*, Guayaquil Press, 1953).

'(viii) gardener's world'
The name of the character in the *The Wheel* is actually Norma. Thanks to María Llorens and Libertad Gills for introducing me to the work of Abel Gance.

'(ix) I don't want to edit your power-point presentations anymore'
'Now I'm ready to close my eyes *C'mon'* and 'I loose my heart on the burning sands' are excerpted from The Stooges' 1969 song 'I Wanna Be Your Dog'.

'Clouds'
'The heath was alight' references Jean Genet's 'Montmartre was aflame'. See: *Our Lady of the Flowers*, Trans. Bernard Frechtman. Olympia Press (2004) p. 79.

'(xi) adding the details left out of the original message*'
*For the artist's comments see: Joe Davis, 'Microvenus', *Art Journal*, Vol. 55, No. 1, Contemporary Art and the Genetic Code (Spring, 1996), p. 73.

'(xii) this is the first account: there were neither animals, birds, fishes, crabs, trees, stones, caves, ravines, grasses, nor forests, there was only the sky – the surface had not yet appeared'

'Miss Chicago and the California Girls' refers to a work produced by Judy Chicago, Faith Wilding, Cay Lang, Vanalyne Green, Dori Atlantis and Sue Bond during the Feminist Art Program at Fresno State College, North America, in 1971.

'The Project'
'Freedom as the absence of impediments of motion' refers to Thomas Hobbes' characterisation of 'freedom or liberty' as 'the absence of opposition to motion' (see: *Leviathan,* Hackett, (1994). p. 136); 'As when a stone lies' references John Locke's 'he is not at liberty in this action, but undergoes as much necessity of moving as a stone that falls', which can be found in Book II, Chapter XXI 'Of Power' (see: *An Essay Concerning Human Understanding*, W. Sharpe and Son, (1823) p. 113); 'I can plunge foaming and gushing' is excerpted from Arthur Schopenhauer, *Prize Essay on the Freedom of the Will*, Cambridge University Press (1999) p. 36; 'I can rise freely as a stream of water' refers to Friedrich Nietzsche's 'thus live the waves' (see: 'Will and Wave', Book IV. Section 310, *The Gay Science*. Trans. Walter Kaufmann. Random House (1974) p. 247).

'Exercises in Memory'
I have excerpted and translated three lines out of order from Eileen Myles' '#10 Ball' (see: *Snowflakes*, Wave Books, (2012) p. 37): 'And a light going out.' 'Do we really know everything about oil?' 'All of us and everyone, the ball we are ontop of'.

'Sketch for 'X' as Excess'
The sentence structure borrows from open source visual programming language Pure Data

and Processing. Thanks to University of the Arts Guayaquil New Media colleague Christian Proaño for introducing me to the basics in 2016.

'Three of Your Shoes and Three of Your Moons (or a Review of 'The Passion According to Carol Rama')' The last lines of this poem reference Paul B. Preciado's 'The Phantom Limb: Carol Rama and the History of Art' (see: *The Passion According to Carol Rama* (Exh. Cat), Museu d'Art Contemporani Barcelona, 2015).

## ACKNOWLEDGEMENTS

Thank you to the editors of *Ambit, datableedzine, Hysteria, Lemony Lemons, Lighthouse Journal* and *Magma* for first publishing some of the poems in this collection.

Thank you to the editors at Eyewear and Vahni Capildeo for making the publishing of this book possible.

Thank you to the following people and collectives for the conversations, teachings and in some case revisions that contributed to the forming of these poems:

Anyely Marín Cisneros, Cal Janet, Cate Myddleton-Evans, Dalida María Benfield, Dani Medina, Dunya Kalantery, Helena Rice, Imogen Cassels, Jack Underwood, Jane Draycott, Lucy Close, Luke Oliver, Madeleine Stack, Maya de Paula Hanika, Meri Torras, Paul B. Preciado, Sam Close, Theophilus Kwek, and Ybelice Briceño.

## ◻◻ EYEWEAR PUBLISHING

TITLES INCLUDE

EYEWEAR
POETRY

**ELSPETH SMITH** DANGEROUS CAKES
**CALEB KLACES** BOTTLED AIR
**GEORGE ELLIOTT CLARKE** ILLICIT SONNETS
**BARBARA MARSH** TO THE BONEYARD
**DON SHARE** UNION
**SHEILA HILLIER** HOTEL MOONMILK
**SJ FOWLER** THE ROTTWEILER'S GUIDE TO THE DOG OWNER
**JEMMA BORG** THE ILLUMINATED WORLD
**KEIRAN GODDARD** FOR THE CHORUS
**COLETTE SENSIER** SKINLESS
**ANDREW SHIELDS** THOMAS HARDY LISTENS TO LOUIS ARMSTRONG
**JAN OWEN** THE OFFHAND ANGEL
**SEAN SINGER** HONEY & SMOKE
**HESTER KNIBBE** HUNGERPOTS
**MEL PRYOR** SMALL NUCLEAR FAMILY
**TONY CHAN** FOUR POINTS FOURTEEN LINES
**MARIA APICHELLA** PSALMODY
**ALICE ANDERSON** THE WATERMARK
**BEN PARKER** THE AMAZING LOST MAN
**MARION MCCREADY** MADAME ECOSSE
**MARIELA GRIFFOR** DECLASSIFIED
**MARK YAKICH** THE DANGEROUS BOOK OF POETRY FOR PLANES
**HASSAN MELEHY** A MODEST APOCALYPSE
**KATE NOAKES** PARIS, STAGE LEFT
**U.S. DHUGA** THE SIGHT OF A GOOSE GOING BAREFOOT
**TERENCE TILLER** THE COLLECTED POEMS
**MATTHEW STEWART** THE KNIVES OF VILLALEJO
**PAUL MULDOON** SADIE AND THE SADISTS
**JENNA CLAKE** FORTUNE COOKIE
**TARA SKURTU** THE AMOEBA GAME
**MANDY KAHN** GLENN GOULD'S CHAIR
**CAL FREEMAN** FIGHT SONGS
**TIM DOOLEY** WEEMOED
**MATTHEW PAUL** THE EVENING ENTERTAINMENT
**NIALL BOURKE** DID YOU PUT THE WEASELS OUT?
**USHA KISHORE** IMMIGRANT
**LEAH UMANSKY** THE BARBAROUS CENTURY
**STEVE KRONEN** HOMAGE TO MISTRESS OPPENHEIMER
**FAISAL MOHYUDDIN** THE DISPLACED CHILDREN OF DISPLACED CHILDREN
**ALEX HOUEN** RING CYCLE
**COLIN DARDIS** THE X OF Y
**JAMES FINNEGAN** HALF-OPEN DOOR
**SOHINI BASAK** WE LIVE IN THE NEWNESS OF SMALL DIFFERENCES
**MICHAEL WILSON** BEDLAM'S BEST & FINEST
**GALE BURNS** MUTE HOUSE
**REBECCA CLOSE** VALID, VIRTUAL, VEGETABLE REALITY
**KEN EVANS** TRUE FORENSICS
**ALEX WYLIE** SECULAR GAMES